Pegasus Princesses

STAR'S GAZE

Pegasus Princesses

STAR'S GAZE

Emily Bliss

illustrated by Sydney Hanson

BLOOMSBURY
CHILDREN'S BOOKS
NEW YORK   LONDON   OXFORD   NEW DELHI   SYDNEY

BLOOMSBURY CHILDREN'S BOOKS
Bloomsbury Publishing Inc., part of Bloomsbury Publishing Plc
1385 Broadway, New York, NY 10018

BLOOMSBURY, BLOOMSBURY CHILDREN'S BOOKS, and the Diana logo
are trademarks of Bloomsbury Publishing Plc

First published in the United States of America in March 2022
by Bloomsbury Children's Books

Bloomsbury books may be purchased for business or promotional use. For information on bulk
purchases please contact Macmillan Corporate and Premium Sales Department at
specialmarkets@macmillan.com

Library of Congress Cataloging-in-Publication Data
Names: Bliss, Emily, author. | Hanson, Sydney, illustrator.
Title: Star's gaze / by Emily Bliss ; illustrated by Sydney Hanson.
Description: New York : Bloomsbury Children's Books, 2022. |
Series: Pegasus princesses ; 4 | Audience: Grades 2–3.
Summary: It's Lucinda's birthday, and Princess Star has planned a spectacular surprise for the
pegasus princesses' winged pet cat, but as soon as they start decorating, mooncat mayhem erupts.
Will Clara and Star be able to save the party?—Provided by publisher.
Identifiers: LCCN 2021044380 (print) | LCCN 2021044381 (e-book)
ISBN 978-1-5476-0841-6 (paperback) • ISBN 978-1-5476-0843-0 (e-book)
Subjects: CYAC: Winged horses—Fiction. | Princesses—Fiction. | Birthdays—Fiction. |
Surprise—Fiction. | Magic—Fiction. | Imaginary creatures—Fiction.
Classification: LCC PZ7.1.B633 St 2022 (print) | LCC PZ7.1.B633 (e-book) |
DDC [Fic]—dc23
LC record available at https://lccn.loc.gov/2021044380
LC e-book record available at https://lccn.loc.gov/2021044381

Book design by John Candell
Typeset by Westchester Publishing Services
Printed in the U.S.A.
2 4 6 8 10 9 7 5 3 1

To find out more about our authors and books visit www.bloomsbury.com
and sign up for our newsletters.

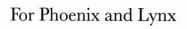

For Phoenix and Lynx

Pegasus Princesses
STAR'S GAZE

Chapter One

"It definitely needs another stripe," Clara Griffin said, picking up a black marker from her family's living room carpet. She pulled off the cap and stepped toward the spaceship she and her younger sister, Miranda, had made from a giant cardboard box. Balancing on her tiptoes, Clara colored in a thick black stripe that started

at the tip of the rocket's pointed nose and ended just above a triangular, tinfoil fin.

"That looks perfect," Miranda said, taking a few steps back to admire the rocket.

"This stripe is magic," Clara explained. "It gives the astronauts inside the spaceship x-ray vision. And this star," Clara continued, outlining a five-pointed star with the marker, "gives the astronauts the ability to speak Gonglepondilglish."

"What's Gonglepondilglish?" Miranda asked, raising her eyebrows.

"It's the language that the Gongles speak on Planet Pondilg," Clara said. "What color do you think we should use to fill in the star?"

"How about pink?" Miranda suggested.

Clara nodded. She put the cap back on the black marker and surveyed the rest of the markers scattered on the floor. She saw red, orange, yellow, green, blue, teal, brown, and purple markers, but no pink. And then she remembered why. The day before, Clara had collected every pink marker in the house, taken them up to her bedroom, and used them to build a space station for her Popsicle-stick pegasus figures.

"I'll go get the pink markers," Clara said.

She dashed out of the living room, galloped up the stairs and down the hall, burst into her bedroom—and nearly tripped over a drawer she had emptied out and filled with a playground for her pegasus figures. She had made a swing set from a bent metal clothes hanger and string, a merry-go-round from a kitchen salad spinner, and a seesaw from two avocado mashers taped together and balanced on top of a saltshaker. Clara leaped forward over the drawer playground and stepped over a stack of papers covered in pictures of pegasus astronauts. She kneeled in front of a giant silver moon she had made by wrapping three layers of tin foil around her mother's exercise ball. On top of the moon was the space station, built out of pink markers and masking tape. Clara grabbed up the markers and peeled off the tape. As she turned to leave the room, she heard a high-pitched humming noise.

Clara paused. At first she thought the noise might be her father running the blender in the kitchen or her mother turning on the lawn mower outside. But the noise was softer and higher than the blender or the lawn mower. And it was coming from somewhere much closer: underneath Clara's bed!

Clara grinned with excitement. She reached under her bed and pulled out a shoebox she had decorated with paint, glitter, and sequins. She flipped open the box. Inside was a large silver feather. The feather hummed louder and louder. Glittery light shot up and down its spine. The feather

had been a gift from the pegasus princesses—eight royal pegasus sisters who ruled over the Wing Realm, a magical world in which all the creatures had wings. Each pegasus princess was a different color and had a unique magical power. Silver Princess Mist could turn invisible. Teal Princess Aqua could breathe underwater and make magic bubbles. Peach Princess Flip could do a special somersault and turn into any animal. Black Princess Star had extraordinary senses. Pink Princess Rosetta—Rosie for short—could speak and understand any language. Green Princess Stitch could sew, knit, or crochet anything. Purple Princess Dash could instantly transport herself anywhere in the Wing Realm. And white Princess Snow could make winter weather and freeze any liquid.

When the pegasus princesses wanted to invite Clara to the Wing Realm for a special occasion, they made the feather hum and shimmer—just the way it was humming and shimmering now! To visit the

Wing Realm, all Clara had to do was bring the feather to a special clearing in the woods surrounding her family's house.

Clara stood up and jumped with excitement. Holding the feather in one hand and the pink markers in the other, she sidled around the moon, hopped over her drawings, and took a giant step over the drawer playground. She was halfway through her bedroom doorway when she looked down and realized she was still wearing the astronaut costume she and her sister had made out of bubble wrap, some garbage bags, and silver duct tape. Clara loved her space suit, but she didn't want to wear it to the Wing Realm, where it might get torn

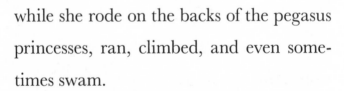

while she rode on the backs of the pegasus princesses, ran, climbed, and even sometimes swam.

Clara carefully took off her space suit. Underneath she was wearing pink corduroy pants decorated with black stars, a white T-shirt with the silhouette of a silver moon on the front, and bright orange socks. Clara slid her feet into her light green canvas sneakers, tucked the magic feather into her pants pocket, and grabbed the pink markers again. She sprinted out of her room, along the hall, down the stairs two steps at a time, and into the living room.

Clara handed her sister the markers and said, "I'll be right back." Time in the human world froze while Clara was in the Wing Realm, so even if she spent hours with the pegasus princesses, Miranda would think she had been away for only a few minutes.

Miranda frowned. "Why did you take off your spacesuit? Aren't we still playing astronauts?" she asked.

"We are definitely still playing astronauts," Clara said. "I just need to collect some pebbles from the woods to use as buttons for the inside of the rocket. I'll put my spacesuit on again as soon as I'm back."

Miranda nodded. "See you in a minute," she said, turning to the star on the side of the spaceship and coloring it in with a bright pink marker.

Clara raced out the back door, across

her yard, and into the woods. She leaped over the creek where she and Miranda liked to make potions. She pulled the magic feather from her pocket and jogged down a hill and into a clearing with a large pine tree.

Glittery light swirled in front of her. A green velvet armchair with large silver wings on its back appeared. The armchair jumped into the air and did a somersault.

Clara giggled. "Hello, chair," she said. "It's nice to see you too."

The chair hopped from side to side. It leaped to Clara, nudged her two times, spun in a circle, and fluttered its wings as it waited.

Clara patted the chair's back and slipped

the silver feather into her pocket. She sat down and said, "Take me to Feather Palace, please."

The chair jumped onto a pine tree bough and bounced up and down. It soared upward, skidded across the top of Clara's house's brick chimney, and sprang straight up into the sky. Clara clutched the chair's arms as everything went pitch black and the chair began to spin, faster and faster. Then Clara and the chair landed with a clatter on a tile floor.

Chapter Two

Clara sucked in her breath as she admired the front hall of Feather Palace. Painted portraits of the eight pegasus princesses and their pet cat, Lucinda, hung on the magenta walls. Chandeliers cast sparkling light on the black tile floors. Pegasus fountains spouted rainbow water. Pegasus sculptures reared up, wings outstretched, from pedestals. In the center of the room, arranged in a half-circle, were the pegasus princesses' eight thrones. Lucinda's sofa—silver with a back shaped like a cat head—was pushed up against Star's throne. And on it Lucinda lay curled in a tight ball, fast asleep.

Clara looked around the front hall for the pegasus princesses. And then she spotted them next to an open window, huddled around what looked like a purple telescope with eight eyepieces. For a few

seconds, Clara watched her friends. And then she called out, "Hello!"

The pegasus princesses jumped in surprise and turned around. As soon as they saw Clara, they reared up, whinnied, and galloped over to her.

"I'm thrilled you're here," Star said, hopping from side to side. "You've arrived just in time."

"Welcome back, human friend," Mist said, trotting in a circle around Clara.

"We've been hoping you would come," Aqua said.

"We have a fun afternoon planned," Dash whispered.

Rosie nodded.

Flip winked.

Stitch and Snow swished their tails.

"I can't wait to tell you what we're doing this afternoon," Star said in a soft voice. "But I'm going to have to whisper it into your ear so *someone*—" Star paused and glanced over at Lucinda, who was still asleep, "doesn't hear. Every once in a while, she pretends to be asleep."

The other seven pegasus princesses grinned and nodded.

Star leaned up to Clara's ear and whispered, "Today is Lucinda's birthday, and I have organized a surprise party for her. Would you like to join us?"

"Yes!" Clara whispered in a voice that

was a little too loud. Clara blushed. She had never been good at whispering.

Star laughed. "I had a feeling you'd say yes," she said. "Are you ready for the best part?"

Clara's eyes widened. She nodded.

"We are holding the party with Lucinda's six cousins, the mooncats, on the Catmoon," Star whispered.

Clara raised her eyebrows. "What is the Catmoon?" she asked.

"It's the Wing Realm's very own moon. We were just looking at it through the octogoloctoscope," Star said, now using her normal voice. "Would you like to see it?"

"Definitely," Clara said.

"Come right this way," Star said, and

she trotted over to the instrument Clara had thought looked like a telescope. "We used to have a normal monogoloctoscope with just one eyepiece," Star explained. "But my sisters and I spent so much time arguing over whose turn it was to use it that we decided to get this one. Pick any eyepiece and look through it."

Clara leaned toward one of the octo-goloctoscope's eyepieces. She closed her left eye and looked through it with her right eye. Clara sucked in her breath with delight. Hanging against a dark lavender backdrop was a silver ball with two mountains that looked like cat ears and two giant green lakes that looked like cat eyes.

"Do you see it?" Star asked.

"Yes," Clara said. "I had no idea the Wing Realm even had a moon."

Star leaned toward Clara's ear and whispered, "We told Lucinda we're all traveling to the Catmoon this afternoon to help her cousins clean their castle. She's irritated she has to do chores on her birthday. She'll be surprised when she discovers we're throwing a party for her instead."

"Clara?" a sleepy voice purred. "Is that you?"

Clara turned away from the octogoloctoscope and skipped over to Lucinda, who was stretching and yawning. "Happy birthday, Lucinda," Clara said, kneeling next to Lucinda and scratching behind her ears.

"Thank you," Lucinda said, purring. Then she sat up and frowned. "Can you believe the pegasus princesses and my cousins are making me clean on my birthday?" she sniffed. "It's bound to be the worst birthday ever."

"That sounds miserable," Clara said, shaking her head. "I'm so sorry. If I'd known it was your birthday I would have tried to convince the pegasus princesses to at least hold a small party for you."

"They say they're too busy for a party," Lucinda said, flashing an annoyed look at Star.

"I'm sorry, Lucinda, but the mooncats' castle is dirty," Star said. "We just can't wait another day to clean it."

Rosie shook her head. "We'll be cleaning for hours. There's no time for a party."

Stitch, Snow, and Dash nodded.

"It's too bad we can't celebrate your birthday this year," Aqua said.

"Next year, maybe we can try to have a party," Mist said.

Lucinda frowned. "What I'd really like is a guessing game birthday party," she said. "I've told you that a million times. But no one seems to have listened."

"What did you say?" Star asked.

"See?" Lucinda said, looking at Clara. "No one listens to me. At least you're here to make things slightly more festive." Lucinda grinned. "Will you play a guessing game with me? Please?"

Clara looked at Star. "Is there time for one guessing game before we go clean the castle?" she asked.

"In just a minute, Clara and I have to leave for the Catmoon to get all the brooms, mops, and feather dusters organized," Star said. "But there's time for one quick game."

"How about," Lucinda suggested, "if I guess your favorite fruit in three guesses."

"Okay," Clara said.

Lucinda flew into the air, did a somersault, and touched her cool, pink nose to the tip of Clara's nose. "I've got it!" she said. "Is it lurdivicto?"

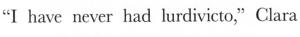
"I have never had lurdivicto," Clara
said.

"Rats!" Lucinda said. "Lurdivicto is a
very good fruit. You should try it sometime.
How about poppletoppleberries?"

"I haven't had those, either," Clara said.

"Double rats!" Lucinda said. She
zoomed in a circle and landed on Clara's

sneakers. "I'll get it this time. How about crapplegrock?"

"I haven't tried crapplegrock, either," Clara said. "I'm afraid the answer is mango."

"Triple rats!" Lucinda said. "What in the world is mango?"

"It sounds more like the name of a dance than a fruit," Star said.

"Or the name of a special hat," suggested Snow.

"Or even the name of a flying scooter," Dash added.

"But definitely not like a fruit," Mist said.

The pegasus princesses and Lucinda shook their heads in wonder. Clara giggled.

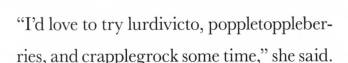
"I'd love to try lurdivicto, poppletoppleber-ries, and crapplegrock some time," she said.

"Well," Star said with a stern face. "You absolutely will not be able to try them this afternoon. We have a job to do on the Catmoon, and there will be no opportuni-ties for fun or snacks. Clara, let's go get to work."

Clara bit her lip to keep from laughing.

Star kneeled, and Clara climbed onto her back. Star looked at her sisters and said, "I'll meet you at the mooncats' castle in two hours."

"I'll come a little early to help organize the mops," Rosie said.

Lucinda looked at Star and Clara. "Can

I come with you?" she asked. "I'd love extra time with Clara and my cousins."

The pegasus princesses exchanged nervous looks.

"Um, well," Star began, "I'd love for you to join us but there might not be room in the rocket for the three of us."

"I could sit on Clara's lap," Lucinda suggested.

"It's just that—" Star began.

"Lucinda," Aqua said, smiling enthusiastically, "I have plenty of room for you to ride to the Catmoon with me in my rocket. We can leave really soon. But first, want to play ten guessing games? I'll give you thirty guesses for each one!"

Lucinda purred with delight and scampered over to Aqua.

Star winked at her sisters and galloped toward the front doors of the palace. The doors swung open to reveal a clear blue sky and an ocean of green treetops below. Star leaped out through the doors and soared into the sky.

Chapter Three

For a moment, Clara turned around and admired Feather Palace. The castle, which looked like two silver wings, sparkled in the sun.

"I feel a little bad that Lucinda is so unhappy about her birthday," Star said. "But she loves surprises and she loves guessing games. I think she'll be ecstatic when she sees what we have planned."

"Will there be guessing games at the party?" Clara asked.

"Oh yes," Star said. "The mooncats and my sisters and I all worked together to get Lucinda a special gift that's perfect for anyone who loves guessing games. It's a gromplesnocker. There will be as many guessing games as Lucinda and her cousins want to play."

Clara was about to ask what a gromple-snocker was when Star said, "If you look straight up, you can just make out the rocket launch cloud."

Clara looked upward and squinted. Sure enough, she saw a black, glittery cloud. The cloud grew bigger and bigger as Star flew higher and higher. "In the human world, do you keep your spaceships on a cloud, too?" Star asked.

Clara giggled. "I don't have my own spaceship in the human world," she said.

"What?" Star said. "Really?"

"Really," Clara said.

"Do you just borrow someone's when you need one?"

"Actually," Clara said, "I've never been in a spaceship before, and I don't know anyone who has."

Star paused in stunned silence. "What do you do when you need to visit a moon?"

"This will be my first time going to a moon," Clara said.

"That is incredible," Star gasped. "Well, in that case, I feel honored to host your first rocket trip. Luckily, we're almost to the launch cloud."

Star flew up to the black glittery cloud and landed right next to a line of eight pegasus-sized spaceships. There was a silver spaceship that said MIST on its side, a teal spaceship that said Aqua, a peach spaceship that said Flip, a black spaceship that said Star, a pink spaceship that said Rosie, a white spaceship that said Snow, a green spaceship that said Stitch, and a lavender spaceship that said Dash on its side.

Star galloped over to her shiny, black rocket and kneeled. Clara slid off Star's back.

Star lifted her front hoof and tapped the side of the rocket three times. A door

appeared. Star tapped the rocket twice. The door swung open to reveal a black velvet armchair and a console with blinking black and purple buttons, yellow and blue levers, flashing maps, and green dials.

"Wow," Clara whispered. "That's amazing."

"I had a feeling you'd like it," Star said with a wink. "Now we need to see if we can both fit inside."

Star leaped into the rocket and onto the armchair. She scooted all the way to one side and said, "Come on in."

Clara climbed into the rocket and squeezed into the space next to Star, so the pegasus's wing brushed against Clara's shoulder.

"We fit perfectly," Star said, smiling. "Pull that blue lever next to your knee to close the door. Then push the purple button to start the rocket."

Clara wrapped her fingers around the lever and pulled it toward her. The door swung closed. She pressed the purple button. The rocket made a soft, humming noise.

"Now, press the black button five times and pull on the yellow lever," Star said. "That tells the rocket to take us to the Catmoon."

Clara counted out loud as she pushed the black button five times. Then she pulled on the yellow lever.

The rocket swayed back and forth. It hopped up and down. It spun in a circle. And then it shot upward. Clara and Star stared out a small, oval window. Clara watched as the rocket zoomed through clouds, pink and yellow stars, and then a stretch of outer space that glowed a deep shade of lavender. After a few minutes,

Clara spotted the Catmoon in the distance. When the rocket reached the Catmoon's twin mountain peaks, it slowed down and cruised above a jungle of teal and pink trees. Then it landed on a sandy silver beach.

"We're here," Star said excitedly. "Press the purple button and then pull the blue lever."

Clara pressed the button, and the rocket turned off. She pulled on the lever, and the door swung open. Clara turned to jump out of the rocket, but before she could, Star said, "Let me go first so I can check for invisilulls."

"What are invisilulls?" Clara asked.

"Invisible moon creatures," Star explained. "I can only see them if I use my magic. They spend a lot of their time sleeping in the sand, and I want to make sure we don't accidentally trip over one. Want to know why?"

Clara nodded.

"If you trip over one and wake it up, it will start singing a lullaby that will put any creature who can hear it immediately to sleep. They only sing for about twenty minutes. But I'm not really in the mood for a nap right now."

"Neither am I," Clara said.

Star climbed over Clara, accidentally brushing her feathered wing and her tail across Clara's face.

"Sorry about that," Star said. She stepped into the rocket's doorway. The moon, star, and planet design on her tiara sparkled. And then she looked from her left to her right.

"I see just one invisilull," she said. "And it happens to be sleeping right next to the rocket." Star leaped out onto the sand and turned to face Clara. "Do you think you can jump this far?"

Clara stepped over to the rocket door. "Definitely," Clara said. She took a deep breath. She bent her knees. And then she leaped out of the rocket and landed in the silver sand next to Star.

Chapter Four

Clara looked all around her. The sky, strewn with wispy orange clouds, glowed lavender. To her left were two green lakes—the same lakes, Clara figured, that had looked like cat eyes when she gazed through the octogoloctoscope. To her right was the jungle of pink and teal trees.

"This place is amazing," Clara said.

"It's my favorite place in the Wing Realm," Star said. "We have a minute to look around before we need to head to the mooncats' castle to set up the party. Would you like me to show you Lake Limpogim and Lake Mogglewop?"

"Definitely," Clara said.

Star looked toward the closest lake. Her tiara sparkled. "The coast is clear of invisilulls," she said. "Follow me!" Star galloped across the sand, and Clara sprinted after her. They stopped at the edge of a lake that looked like it was full of thick, shiny, green slime. As Clara watched, the slime bubbled and lapped the shore in slow, gentle waves.

"This is Lake Limpogim," Star said. "It's full of imagiputty."

41

"What's imagiputty?" Clara asked.

"I'll show you," Star said with a wink. "Grab a handful and roll it into a ball."

Clara kneeled, reached her hand into the lake, and grabbed a glob of imagiputty. She had expected it to feel cold and sticky, but instead it felt warm and soft.

"Perfect," Star said. "Now hold it in both hands, close your eyes, and imagine a small present you'd like to give Lucinda for her birthday."

Clara shut her eyes. She thought for a moment. And then she imagined a soft, silver, star-shaped pillow for Lucinda's cat sofa in Feather Palace. The imagiputty grew warmer and warmer in Clara's hands. And then she felt it disappear and something soft take its place.

"Now you can look," Star said.

Clara opened her eyes and saw in her hands exactly the same pillow she had imagined.

"That's a perfect gift for Lucinda," Star said. "She'll love it."

"Can you make anything with imagiputty?" Clara asked.

"Anything that isn't alive," Star said.

Clara was thinking about all the things she would like to make out of imagiputty— a pegasus costume, shoes with springs on the soles, her very own monogoloctoscope, buttons for the inside of the rocket she and Miranda made—when she heard a shuffling noise. Clara looked down and noticed a blue, crab-like creature. But instead of a shell, the creature's body looked like broom bristles. It had two eyes on light blue stalks, two filmy blue wings, and two dark blue arms with small brooms on the ends instead of pinchers.

"What is that?" Clara asked as the creature began to sweep silver sand into a small hill.

"That's a bristleblonk," Star said. "They're all over the beaches on the Cat-moon. They're completely harmless."

For a few seconds, Clara and Star watched the bristleblonk as it swept more and more sand into a bigger and bigger pile. When the pile was as tall as Clara's knees, the bristleblonk grunted with delight. It hopped up to the top of the hill, grunted happily, and rolled down the hill. As soon as the bristleblonk reached the bottom of the hill, it climbed back up to the top and rolled down again. The bristleblonk did it again. And again. And again.

"Want to see another creature?" Star asked.

"Absolutely," Clara said.

Star turned toward the other lake. "Let me just look for invisilulls before we head over to Lake Mogglewop." Her tiara sparkled. "There's one that's about to hop right in front of us," she said. "Let's wait just a moment."

Clara nodded. "What does an invisilull look like?" she asked.

"They look like bright orange rabbits with purple antlers, purple wings, and purple hooves," Star said.

Clara smiled as she imagined the invisilull in her mind.

"Okay," Star said, her tiara sparkling again. "All clear. Now I'll show you the snogglesnurps."

Clara skipped in the sand alongside Star until they came to the shore of Lake Mogglewop, which was full of small green marbles. The marbles churned and swirled. And then, to Clara's surprise, a fountain of marbles spurted up into the air. Clara opened her mouth to ask a question, but before she could speak, a purple creature with a long, tube-shaped snout and a tiny, ball-shaped head appeared. Its body looked to Clara like a plum-colored, deflated beach ball with small, clear wings. Two yellow duck feet poked out from its belly.

"Is that a snogglesnurp?" Clara whispered in amazement.

"It sure is," Star said. "Watch what it does now."

Clara and Star stared at the snogglesnurp. It waddled around for a few seconds on top of the lake. Then it dipped its snout into the marbles. It made a loud slurping noise as its body grew bigger and bigger. It was sucking in the marbles! When the snugglesnurp's belly was full, it grinned, rolled onto its back, made a happy snorting noise, and pointed its snout straight upward. A stream of marbles shot out of its snout into the air until its body was tiny again.

"That was amazing," Clara said.

"I thought you'd like it," Star said. "Lake

Mogglewop is full of snogglesnurps. I wish we could keep watching them. But I think we'd better hike to the mooncats' castle to get ready for Lucinda's party. I have a feeling Lucinda's cousins might need a little help cleaning and decorating."

Clara giggled and nodded. If Lucinda's

cousins were anything like Lucinda, Clara suspected that she and Star might end up doing all the work.

Star's tiara sparkled as she looked toward the jungle. "No invisilulls! Let's go!"

Clara and Star walked together across the sand and into the jungle. They found a narrow path that wove through a grove of trees. The path made a sharp right turn into a clearing. And there Clara saw a silver castle shaped like a cat head. It had two triangular towers shaped like cat ears, two green glass windows that looked like cat eyes, and a giant pink cat nose where Clara would have expected a door.

"Let's go in," Star said, rearing up with excitement. She galloped up to the pink cat

nose, crouched down, and pushed with her head against it. To Clara's surprise, it swung open like a giant cat flap. For a moment, Clara giggled with delight. Then she dropped to her hands and knees and crawled through the cat flap into the castle.

Chapter Five

Clara found herself in a front hall that was almost as messy as her bedroom. Twisted, shredded streamers draped over silver cat-head sofas, crisscrossed the white tile floors, and littered the floor in tangled clumps. Strewn across a cat-shaped shag rug were party hats and balloons that had yet to be blown up. A white banner lay on the floor with

the letters *H-A-P-P* painted in purple. Next
to the banner was an overturned glass jar,
a puddle of purple paint, and many purple
paw prints. Standing next to the rug was
what looked to Clara like a giant gumball
machine. On its top was a clear glass globe
full of bouncing, bean-sized, black balls.

Encased in the
tower below
the globe was
a spiral chute.
At its base was a
silver button and
a small open-
ing. The front
hall was such

a mess that it took Clara a few seconds to notice that in a patch of sunlight below an open window, six cats, all silver and winged, slept curled up together.

"I'm glad we got here early," Star whispered to Clara. "I thought it would be messy. But this is an even bigger mess than I expected. At least the cats remembered to get the gromplesnocker." Star nodded to the thing that looked to Clara like a gumball machine.

"How does it work?" Clara asked.

"I think I'd better show you *before* we wake up the mooncats. Gromps tend to make Wing Realm cats a little . . ." Star's voice trailed off and she flashed a smile at

Clara. "Well, let's just say the cats find the gromps exciting."

Clara giggled.

Star trotted over to the gromple-snocker and gazed down at the button. "Push that once," she said. "And make sure you don't hold it down for more than half a second."

Clara skipped over to the gromple-snocker. She kneeled, pushed the silver button, and released it quickly. One gromp rolled down the spiral chute and flew out the opening. As soon as it landed on the floor, it began to bounce and jump, higher and higher, faster and faster. As it bounced off the floor, the ceiling, and the walls, it yelled,

"Guess my favorite flower! Guess my favorite flower! Guess my favorite flower!"

Clara blinked in surprise.

"Margleclops?" Star guessed. "Proglets?"

The gromp kept bouncing and yelling.

"Um," Clara said, trying to remember flowers she had encountered in the Wing Realm. "Ear-flowers?"

The gromp kept bouncing and yelling.

"Largostopples?" Star tried.

"Two-lips?" Clara suggested.

The gromp still kept bouncing and yelling.

"Lusterflops?" Star suggested.

As soon as the word came out of Star's

mouth, the gromp vanished. In an instant, vases full of shiny gold flowers that looked like big, floppy roses appeared on all the window sills and along the walls.

"Wow," Clara said. "That was amazing!"

"We can use the gromplesnocker more during Lucinda's party," Star said. "But I think we'd better wake up the mooncats and see if we can get them to help us clean and decorate. Maybe now that they've had a nap, they'll be able to focus on getting ready."

Star looked at the sleeping cats and smiled. "We're here!" she called out in a loud voice.

The cats rolled over. They swished their tails. They opened one eye and then the other. When they saw Star and Clara they purred with excitement, flipped onto all fours, and rushed over to Clara.

"You must be Clara," a cat exclaimed, fluttering her wings and doing a flip in the air.

"You're finally here," another cat purred, rubbing Clara's ankles.

"Cousin Lucinda has told us all about you," another cat said, flapping his wings and landing on Clara's head.

"We've been so excited to finally meet you," two cats said at the same time. They flew up to Clara's face and sniffed her nose.

"I'm glad to be here," Clara said. "It sounds like you already know my name is Clara. Will you tell me your names?"

The cats proudly took turns meowing their names:

"Letitia."

"Langston."

"Loretta."

"Leander."

"Lizbeth."

"Ludwig."

When they finished, Clara said, "It's a pleasure to meet you."

Ludwig looked over at Star and sighed. "We started getting ready for the party," he said.

"We meant to finish cleaning up and decorating," Lizbeth explained.

"I even worked on the happy birthday

banner for a full two minutes," Loretta said.

"But we got a little—" Langston said.

"Distracted," all six cats said at once.

"Streamers are just really fun to unroll," Letitia confessed.

"And shred," Langston said.

"And twist," Leander said.

"And bat around the room," Lizbeth said.

Loretta and Ludwig nodded in agreement.

"I'm glad you had fun with the streamers," Star said, laughing. "They look a little too shredded to hang on the walls. But we can still have a party without streamers.

Right now we really do need to work together to get ready."

The cats nodded.

Star looked around the room and thought for a moment. "Leander and Loretta, why don't you finish the banner?" she suggested. "Langston and Lizbeth, could you get all the streamers and put them in another room? Ludwig and Letitia, how about if you work on cleaning up all those paw prints? And Clara, since you have hands, why don't you blow up the balloons and tidy up the party hats?"

"We'll get right to work," Loretta said as she and Leander strutted over to the banner.

"Nothing will come between us and getting ready for the party," Leander said in a confident voice.

"We absolutely will not get distracted," Langston said as he and Lizbeth used their paws to gather the streamers.

"Focus is my new middle name," Lizbeth said.

"We'll be ready for the party in no time," Ludwig said as he and Letitia rubbed the tips of their tails against the paw prints to clean them up.

Clara set down Lucinda's pillow on a window sill and skipped over to the rug. She sat down and stacked up all the party hats. Next, she picked up a pink balloon, held the opening to her mouth, and blew. She tied a knot in the bottom, and began to blow up a blue one.

"Excellent work, everyone," Star said. "I'll start dusting." She galloped over to a window sill and swept her tail back and forth.

As Clara tied a knot in a blue balloon, she heard a shuffling noise behind her. She turned around to see that Leander, Langston, Letitia, Lizbeth, Loretta, and Ludwig were gathered in a tight circle around a tangle of streamers. Their tails swished back and forth as they batted the streamers with their paws.

"Um, mooncats?" Clara said.

The cats did not turn around. Instead,

Lizbeth lunged forward, picked up the tangled clump of streamers in her mouth, and bolted across the room. For a moment, Leander, Langston, Letitia, Loretta, and Ludwig watched Lizbeth. Their green cat eyes widened in excitement. And then they bounded after her. In the blink of an eye, all six cats were sprinting in faster and faster circles around the room.

"Mooncats!" Star called out. "Stop! Stop right now!"

But the mooncats didn't stop. Instead, Lizbeth leaped into the center of the room and pounced on the gromplesnocker's silver button. A split second later, Leander, Langston, Letitia, Loretta, and Ludwig landed right on top of Lizbeth. Clara gasped as all the gromps came pouring down the spiral chute and shot out the opening into the room.

Gromps bounced off the floors, the walls, and the ceiling. At first, Clara could hear what they were yelling: "Guess my favorite kind of cupcake!" "Guess my favorite color streamer!" "Guess my favorite birthday music!" "Guess my favorite party drink!" "Guess my favorite party snack!" "Guess my favorite party game!" "Guess my favorite birthday present!" and "Guess my favorite color disco light!" Soon there were so many gromps yelling what to guess, and the sound of them bouncing was so loud, that it all sounded like noisy chaos. Clara didn't think the room could get any louder. But then the cats began to chase after the gromps, meowing loudly the whole time.

Clara and Star looked at each other. Clara covered her ears with her hands. Star flattened her ears against her head, bolted across the room, and threw herself out the cat flap door. Clara took a deep breath and ran after her.

Chapter Six

Outside the mooncats' castle, Star's eyes filled with tears. "Oh no," she whimpered. "What are we going to do?"

Clara took a long deep breath. "I'm not sure," she admitted.

"There is no way we can hold Lucinda's surprise party now," Star said, shaking her head. Tears streamed down her cheeks as she added, "Now she'll actually think we didn't care about her birthday."

"Is there any way to get the gromps back into the gromplesnocker?" Clara asked.

Star shook her head. "Once they're out, they bounce around and yell things to guess until someone says the right answer. The glass globe at the top does have a lid that opens." Star furrowed her brow and paused. "But I can't think of any way we could get them to bounce back inside."

Clara heard the sound of wings beating the air. She turned to see Rosie soaring over the jungle toward them. Rosie smiled cheerfully as she landed next to Star and Clara. "Sorry I'm late," she said. "I had trouble getting my spaceship to start.

I can't wait for Lucinda's surprise party. How can I help get ready? Do you want me to—" Rosie looked at Star's and Clara's faces. "Is something wrong?" she asked. "Why are you both standing outside the castle?"

Star sniffled as she told Rosie the whole story of what had happened with the moon-cats, the streamers, and the gromple-snocker. "Oh dear," Rosie said. She trotted over to the cat flap door and poked her head through it. She quickly backed out with her ears flattened against her head. "What a disaster," she said. "That's the noisiest room I've ever been in. We will definitely need to cancel Lucinda's party. Do you want me to take my spaceship back to Feather Palace right now and tell the others not to come?"

"I guess so," Star said, looking down at her hooves.

"Wait," Clara said. "Let's take a few minutes to see if we can think of any way to save the party."

Star and Rosie nodded. Star furrowed her brow and cocked her head to the side as she thought. Rosie bit her lip and tapped her hooves against the ground. Clara took a long deep breath. And then another. She closed her eyes. She thought about the bouncing, shrieking gromps and the excited mooncats. She thought about the two lakes, the invisilulls, the bristleblonk, and the snogglesnurp. She thought about Star's magic senses and Rosie's magical ability to speak and understand any language. And then Clara opened her eyes, hopped from one foot to the other, and said, "I have an idea. I don't know if it will work. But the only way to find out is to try."

"I'll do absolutely anything to save the party," Star said.

"Me too," Rosie said. "Anything at all."

"The first step is we need to go down to Lake Limpogim," Clara said.

"The fastest way to get there is to fly," Rosie said.

"Let's go," Star agreed, kneeling as Clara climbed onto her back. Star and Rosie flapped their wings and lifted into the sky. They soared over the jungle, above

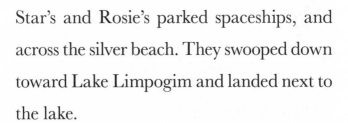

Star's and Rosie's parked spaceships, and across the silver beach. They swooped down toward Lake Limpogim and landed next to the lake.

Star kneeled as Clara slid off her back. Clara skipped over to the bubbling lake, and for a few seconds she watched the slow waves of imagiputty roll to the shore. With both hands she reached into the lake and pulled out the biggest glob of imagiputty she could hold. She rolled the imagiputty into a large ball. She closed her eyes. She imagined five pairs of earmuffs like the ones she and other kids at school wore when their classroom got too loud. In her mind, two pairs were tiny, two pairs were pegasus-sized, and the last pair would fit Clara. She imagined that these particular pairs of earmuffs would work so well that they would block out all sound.

The imagiputty grew warmer and warmer in her hands until it vanished. A split second later, Clara opened her eyes as the five pairs of earmuffs appeared.

"What are those?" Star and Rosie asked at the same time.

"They're called earmuffs," Clara said. "I'll show you how they work when we get back to the castle. But right now, what we need is an invisilull."

"I can help with that," Star said. Her tiara sparkled as she turned to her left. Her eyes widened and she jumped backward. "An invisilull is sniffing your sneakers," she said to Clara.

Clara giggled as she felt something gently poke her leg. She thought it was probably the invisilull's antler. Clara looked at Rosie. "Could you please ask the invisilull to come back to the castle and help us?"

Rosie cocked her head to the side in confusion. But then she smiled. "Clara, if there's one thing I know about you, it's that you have some of the best creative ideas to solve tricky problems. I'll ask the invisilull." The jumble of letters on Rosie's tiara sparkled. And then she sang, "Lalish la la la lishalull lish lalull?"

A high, squeaky voice that came from right in front of them sang back: "Lullish lill lush lush."

Rosie laughed. "The invisilull says no one has ever invited her to a party. She can't wait to join us and help."

"Perfect," Clara said. She thought for a moment. "Do you think she could jump up onto your back so we don't trip over her?"

"I'll ask," Rosie said. Her tiara sparkled and she sang, "Lalisha lish lush lash lalishlash?"

"Lish!" the squeaky voice sang. "Lish! Lish! Lish!"

Rosie giggled. After a second, she said, "There is a very happy invisilull doing a dance on my back."

"Perfect," Clara said, glad to help the invisilull feel included and happy. "Now we need a bristleblonk."

As soon as the words came out of Clara's mouth, a bristleblonk glided across the sand in front of Star's hooves and began to sweep the sand into a small hill. "Should I ask it to come with us to the castle?" Rosie said.

"Yes, please," Clara said.

Rosie's tiara sparkled. "Blinkablonka-bloinka?" she said in a gravelly voice. "Blob-bika blinkotta bronk?"

The bristleblonk stopped sweeping the sand, jumped up, and grunted, "Bloink! Bloink! Bloink! Bloink!"

Rosie laughed. "That bristleblonk is excited to join us." Her tiara sparkled and she grunted, "Blonkobloink blink blonket-bloink invisilull bloinky."

The bristleblonk leaped up onto Rosie's back. "I told it to hop up, and to be careful of my other passenger, the invisilull," Rosie said to Star and Clara with a wink.

"Fantastic," Clara said. "We're almost ready to go back to the castle to put my plan to work. We just need a snogglesnurp."

Star turned and looked at the stretch of sand between them and Lake Mogglewop. Her tiara sparkled. "The coast is clear of invisilulls," she said. "Let's go!"

Star and Rosie galloped toward Lake Mogglewop while Clara sprinted after them. The three stopped at the lake's edge and watched as the green marbles swirled and churned. After a few seconds, a stream of marbles sprayed up into the sky. And then a snogglesnurp crawled out onto the surface of the lake. For a moment, it sniffed the air with its long snout and blinked. Then it waddled toward them.

"I'll ask it to come back to the castle and help us," Rosie said. Her tiara sparkled. And then she quacked, "Snorplepockleprond plonklesnorple snorplesnoop?"

The snogglesnurp's eyes widened. It made a loud, excited quacking noise.

"Snooplepondsnorp invisilull bristleblonk sporpsnoop," Rosie said.

The snogglesnurp jumped into the air, fluttered its wings, and landed behind the bristleblonk. "Well, that was easy," Rosie said.

"Thanks so much," Clara said. "Are you ready to fly back to the castle?"

"I can't wait to see what your plan to

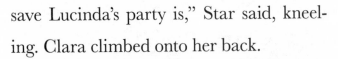

save Lucinda's party is," Star said, kneeling. Clara climbed onto her back.

"I'll fly extra carefully, since I have three passengers," Rosie said, with a wink.

Star and Rosie flapped their wings, flew up into the sky, and headed straight back to the castle.

Chapter Seven

C lara pushed open the castle's pink cat flap and peeked into the front hall. The gromps were still bouncing and yelling. The mooncats were still running laps around the room and meowing loudly. Clara backed out with her hands over her ears.

"Rosie," Clara said, "could you ask the

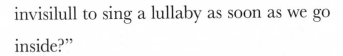

invisilull to sing a lullaby as soon as we go inside?"

"Okay," Rosie said, sounding puzzled by Clara's request. Her tiara sparkled and she sang, "Lalull lull lalalish lull lullaby?"

"Lish!" the invisilull sang out. "Lish! Lish! Lish!"

Clara smiled. "Now we get to try out these earmuffs," she said. She placed the tiny pairs of earmuffs on the bristleblonk and the snogglesnurp. She put the pegasus-sized earmuffs on Rosie and Star. And finally, she put the fifth pair on herself. Clara made a thumbs-up sign for Star and Rosie. They nodded at her with nervous faces.

Clara took a deep breath. She crawled

through the cat flap with Star and Rosie right behind her. To Clara's relief, the ear- muffs worked better than any earmuffs she had ever worn. She couldn't hear the gromps yelling. She couldn't hear the cats meowing. And she couldn't hear the invisi- lull's lullaby even though she knew the invisilull had begun to sing. The gromps stopped bouncing. For a few seconds, they rolled around on the floor. And then they lay completely still. The mooncats slowed from sprinting to walking. And then from walk- ing to standing. Their eyelids drooped. They yawned and rocked back and forth. And then all six mooncats curled up in the center of the rug, closed their eyes, and fell fast asleep.

Clara, Star, and Rosie exchanged hopeful smiles. Clara skipped over to Rosie, picked up the bristleblonk, and put it on the floor. For a few seconds, the bristleblonk's eyes moved in circles as it looked at all the gromps. Then it hurriedly swept up the gromps with its bristle body and bristle hands. After a few minutes, every single gromp was in one large mound. The bristleblonk hopped up the gromp hill and rolled down it. As it hopped to the top of the hill and rolled down again, Clara skipped over to Rosie. She lifted up the snogglesnurp and gently set it down next to the gromp hill. The snogglesnurp sniffed the gromps with its long snout. Then it grinned, dipped its snout into the gromps, and began to inhale them. The gromp hill grew smaller and smaller as the snogglesnurp's body swelled larger and larger. When all the gromps were inside the snogglesnurp, it rolled backward and pointed its snout upward. That's when Clara leaned over, grabbed the snogglesnurp, and raced over to the gromplesnocker.

Star took one look at Clara and galloped over to the gromplesnocker. She used her mouth to lift the lid on top of the glass globe. Clara turned the snogglesnurp upside down so its snout pointed right into the gromple-snocker. A second later, the snogglesnurp was shooting out the gromps. Clara exhaled with relief as she watched the globe fill with gromps and the snogglesnurp's body shrivel up. When the snogglesnurp finished, Star closed the lid.

The plan had worked! Clara hopped up and down with excitement. Star reared up with joy. Rosie flashed a thrilled smile. Then Rosie glanced toward her back and looked at Clara expectantly. Clara paused. And then she realized Rosie wanted her to take the invisilull off her back. Clara skipped over to Rosie and waved her hands slowly in the air above Rosie's back. When her hands touched soft fur, Clara gently found the invisilull's body and picked it up. She placed the invisilull on the windowsill right next to the pillow she planned to give Lucinda.

Clara scratched the invisilull's head

between its ears and antlers for a few seconds. When she turned around, she was surprised to see that Rosie, Star, the bristleblonk, and the snogglesnurp were all working together to clean up the front hall. The bristleblonk was sweeping all the shredded, torn, tangled streamers into a pile. The snogglesnurp was waddling around and sucking up all the purple paint from the tile floor. Rosie was dusting the couches and windowsills with her tail. And Star was using her hooves to make a neat pile of balloons to blow up. Clara skipped over to the balloons. She blew up a red one, an orange one, a yellow one, a green one, a blue one, and then a purple one. Just as she was blowing up the last

balloon—a silver one—she noticed that the gromps in the gromplesnocker were rolling around. After a few seconds, they jumped and hopped. And then they began to bounce all over the inside of the globe, just as they'd been doing when Clara first saw the gromplesnocker.

Clara turned to the mooncats. Leander, Lizbeth, Langston, Loretta, Ludwig, and Letitia yawned and stretched. They opened their eyes and blinked. They swished their tails and purred. Clara bet the invisilull had stopped singing. Clara took off her earmuffs. Sure enough, the lullaby was over. She skipped over to Star and Rosie and pulled off their earmuffs. Then she took the earmuffs off the bristleblonk and the snogglesnurp.

"Thank you so much, Clara," Star said, beaming. "Your idea saved Lucinda's surprise party. She'll be here any minute now."

"It was my pleasure to help," Clara said.

Just then, Clara noticed Lizbeth creeping over to the pile of ruined streamers with an excited look in her eyes. "I think I'll just put those streamers outside for now," Clara said, rushing over and picking them up.

"Good idea," Star said.

Clara ran across the room, dashed out the cat flap, and hid the streamers behind a tree.

When she came back inside, the snogglesnurp waddled up to her and quacked, "Snurpalurp glurp lurpy?"

Clara turned to Rosie, whose tiara sparkled as she listened. Then Rosie smiled and said, "The snogglesnurp wants to help you finish making the happy birthday banner by spraying out paint while you move it around to form the letters."

"What a great idea," Clara said. She picked up the snogglesnurp, skipped over to the banner, and held the snogglesnurp so its snout pointed toward the banner. The snogglesnurp spurted out purple paint as Clara moved the snogglesnurp to paint a *Y*. Then she painted the word *BIRTHDAY*.

Clara looked at Rosie and said, "How do I say thank you in its language?"

"Spurplesnop," Rosie said.

Clara put down the snogglesnurp, smiled, and said, "Spurplesnop."

The snogglesnurp made a delighted quacking sound. Then it waddled over to

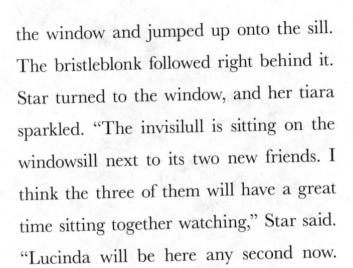

the window and jumped up onto the sill. The bristleblonk followed right behind it. Star turned to the window, and her tiara sparkled. "The invisilull is sitting on the windowsill next to its two new friends. I think the three of them will have a great time sitting together watching," Star said. "Lucinda will be here any second now. I think we're finally ready."

"It really wasn't much work at all getting ready for the party," Langston said, purring as he admired the banner.

"We should host surprise parties more often," Loretta said.

"It was easy-peasy decorating and cleaning," Lizbeth agreed. She sauntered over to the pile of balloons and began to bat them with her paw. Ludwig and Letitia rushed over.

Clara opened her mouth to ask the mooncats not to play with the balloons, when Snow, Mist, Aqua, Flip, Dash, and Stitch rushed in through the cat flap.

Chapter Eight

"**W**e just asked Lucinda to fly back to my spaceship to get a broom," Snow said. "When she gets here, let's all yell *SURPRISE!* and sing Happy Birthday."

"Perfect," Star said.

"The front hall looks amazing," Dash said, admiring the balloons and the banner.

"This is the cleanest and most organized I've ever seen the castle," Aqua declared.

"But weren't there supposed to be streamers?" Stitch asked.

Clara, Rosie, and Star looked at each other and smiled.

"The streamers are a bit of a long story. We'll tell you later," Star said with a wink.

Before anyone could respond, Lucinda burst through the cat flap carrying a small broom in her mouth.

Clara, all six mooncats, and all eight pegasus princesses shouted, "Surprise!" Then they sang Happy Birthday.

Lucinda dropped the broom on the floor with a clatter. She looked at the gromplesnocker, the balloons, and the banner. She looked at her six cousins, the pegasus princesses, the bristleblonk, the snogglesnurp, and Clara. With a delighted purr and a somersault in the air, she said, "My whole life I've dreamed of having a gromplesnocker at my birthday party. I thought today was going to be the worst birthday I've ever had. And now I think it will be the very best."

Clara laughed and scratched Lucinda behind her ears.

"Can we start the guessing games right now?" Lucinda asked.

"Of course," Star said.

Lucinda, Leander, Letitia, Langston, Lizbeth, Ludwig, and Loretta meowed with excitement and raced over to the gromplesnocker.

"There is one really, really important rule," Star said.

"Yes," Rosie said, nodding.

"Only one gromp at a time," Star and Rosie said together.

The cats purred and swished their tails. Lucinda lifted up her paw and quickly tapped the button at the gromplesnocker's base. A single gromp barreled down the chute and shot out into the room. "Guess my favorite fruit! Guess my favorite fruit!" it shouted as it bounced off the floor, the ceiling, and the walls.

The cats' eyes widened and they chased the gromp, calling out, "Lorgmock!" "Rausterlope!" "Quacklepong!" "Neer-onop!" and "Bronkopopper!" When Lucinda shouted, "Lurdivicto!" the gromp vanished, and one platter, one trough, and one small bowl appeared. Each was full of grape-sized, green-and-pink-striped balls.

"Let's keep playing and eat the lurdi-victo later!" Lucinda said.

"Definitely!" Langston and Letitia said.

Leander tapped the button next, and a gromp shot out yelling, "Guess my favorite party snack! Guess my favorite party snack!"

The cats and the pegasus princesses called out, "Jumadaya!" "Flingonapper!" "Clongophoppers!" and "Horntowfronds!" Then Clara said, "Crapplegrock!"

The gromp vanished, and a platter, a trough, and a bowl appeared. This time, they were full of what looked like sliced purple peaches with green dots.

"Let's eat later!" Loretta said.

Ludwig rushed to the gromplesnocker and tapped the button. A gromp shot out yelling, "Guess my favorite party drink! Guess my favorite party drink!"

The cats and the pegasus princesses

called out their guesses: "Finklerade!"
"Norangocola!" "Quintada!" "Lurpleglump
juice!" And then Star tried, "Poppletopple-
berry punch!" The gromp vanished, and
seven cat dishes, a trough, and a cup—all
full of blue, bubbly liquid—appeared.

"I never thought I'd say this," Lucinda
said, "but I'm ready for a break from guessing games. Let's eat and drink!"

The mooncats purred with delight.

"I'm ready for lurdivicto!" Leander
called out.

"Lurdivicto! Lurdivicto!" all seven cats
meowed as they crowded around the platter and began to eat.

"I do love lurdivicto," Star said.

"Me too," Mist, Flip, and Aqua said

as all eight pegasus princesses gathered around the trough.

Clara skipped over to the bowl of lurdivicto. She picked up one of the striped balls, sniffed it, and then, with an excited grin, took a bite. The lurdivicto was the most amazing fruit Clara had ever had—it tasted like a combination of mint candy cane, marshmallows, and bubblegum. Clara finished her lurdivicto just as the cats and pegasus princesses finished theirs.

"Now let's have the crapplegrock!" Lucinda called out, bounding over to the other fruit platter. The six mooncats followed her, and all seven cats began to eat.

The pegasus princesses reared up with excitement and rushed to the trough of crapplegrock and began to devour the fruit.

"Crapplegrock is definitely my favorite fruit!" Dash said, as purple juice dripped down her purple chin.

"Me too!" Snow said, closing her eyes with pleasure.

Clara skipped over to her bowl. She picked up a slice, bit into it—and then immediately spat it out! It tasted like a combination of spoiled sardines, olives, raw garlic, and mayonnaise.

Star looked at her in shock. "You don't like crapplegrock?" she asked.

Clara shook her head vigorously and looked for something to drink to get the taste out of her mouth. She sprinted over to the glass of poppletoppleberry punch and began to drink it. To her relief, it tasted like a combination of root beer and hot chocolate.

Just then, the cats and pegasus princesses finished the crapplegrock. "That was so good!" Lucinda purred.

"It was tremendous!" Aqua said.

The seven cats and the eight pegasus

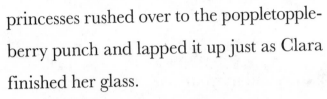

princesses rushed over to the poppletopple-berry punch and lapped it up just as Clara finished her glass.

As they drank, Clara skipped over to the window sill, grabbed the star-shaped pillow she had made as a present for Lucinda, and skipped back to the cats. Lucinda finished her punch and grinned with contentment.

Clara kneeled in front of Lucinda and smiled. "I have a present for you," she said, holding the pillow out.

Lucinda purred. "Thank you so much," she said. "I'll put it on my cat sofa in Feather Palace. I'll think of you every time I put my head on it to take a nap."

Clara scratched Lucinda behind her ears.

Lucinda purred and said, "Now I'm ready for more gromps!"

"More gromps! More gromps!" the mooncats yelled.

That's when Clara realized she was ready to go home. She missed Miranda. She wanted to finish making their spaceship. And she was ready to eat human food.

Clara looked at Star. "I have had a wonderful time with you today. But I'm ready to go back to the human world."

Star smiled. "After you tried the crapple-grock, I had a feeling you might want to go home," she said. "The Catmoon is part of the Wing Realm. Your magic feather works here. You can leave whenever you're ready."

Clara looked at the eight pegasus princesses and the seven cats. "Thank you so much for including me today," Clara said. "I'm going to say goodbye for now and return to the human world."

"Thank you for coming!" Lucinda purred, flying over to Clara and rubbing her ankles.

"Please come back any time," Leander said.

"You're always welcome on the Catmoon," Letitia said.

Langston, Lizbeth, Ludwig, and Loretta purred and jumped onto Clara's head and shoulders.

"Thank you for all your help," Star said.

"Thank you for saving the party," Rosie said.

"Come again soon," Stitch said.

"Goodbye for now, human friend!" Mist said, rearing up.

"Have a wonderful rest of your day," Aqua said.

Clara pulled her feather from her pocket. She wrapped her hands around it and said, "Take me home, please!"

The feather pulled her through the cat flap and lifted her up into the sky. Everything went pitch black and she felt herself spinning and flying. Suddenly, she was sitting under the pine tree in the woods behind her house. For a moment, Clara smiled. She pushed the feather into her pocket and noticed something hard inside. Clara's eyes widened as she pulled out a handful of small green marbles from Lake Mogglewop that would be, she realized, perfect for the spaceship's buttons. Clara hopped up and down with delight and sprinted toward her house with the marbles in her hand, excited to show them to Miranda.

Don't miss our other new high-flying adventure!

Turn the page for a sneak peek ...

Flip galloped into the front hall wearing goggles and a pointy peach wizard's hat with a silver spiral design that matched the gemstone pattern on her tiara. "I'm so glad you're here!" Flip exclaimed, rearing up with excitement. "You've arrived just in time. Welcome back to the Wing Realm."

"Thank you for inviting me," Clara said.

Flip looked at Lucinda. The pegasus cocked her head and smiled. "Are you sure you didn't play any guessing games?" she asked. "Not even one?"

Lucinda sniffed and twitched her tail. "Well, maybe one," she admitted before sauntering over to her cat sofa and curling up in a ball. "Don't mind me," she said between yawns. "I'm due for my morning nap. Her eyelids fluttered and then shut. She let out a loud noise that was half-purr and half-snore.

Clara giggled. Flip shook her head in amusement before she turned to Clara. "I can't wait to tell you what we're doing this afternoon. It's my favorite day of the year. Today is our annual Potion Fair. Teams of creatures from all over the Wing Realm spend the year inventing and perfecting new magic potions. Then we bring them to the fair and share them with each other. Would you like to join us?"

"I would love to join you," Clara said.

"I'm so glad," Flip said. "Especially since this year my sisters and I invented a potion with you in mind."

"Really?" Clara asked.

"Really," Flip said, eyes gleaming. "We invented a flying potion. If you sprinkle it over your head, you'll be able to fly even though you don't have wings."

"That sounds amazing," Clara said.

Emily Bliss, also the author of the Unicorn Princesses series, lives with her winged cat in a house surrounded by woods. From her living room window, she can see silver feathers and green flying armchairs. Like Clara Griffin, she knows pegasuses are real.

Sydney Hanson was raised in Minnesota alongside numerous pets and brothers. She is the illustrator of the Unicorn Princesses series and the picture books *Next to You, Escargot,* and *A Book for Escargot,* among many others. Sydney lives in Los Angeles.

www.sydwiki.tumblr.com